Dear Parents and Educators,

Welcome to Penguin Young Readers! As parents and educators, you know that each child develops at his or her own pace—in terms of speech, critical thinking, and, of course, reading. Penguin Young Readers recognizes this fact. As a result, each Penguin Young Readers book is assigned a traditional easy-to-read level (1–4) as well as a Guided Reading Level (A–P). Both of these systems will help you choose the right book for your child. Please refer to the back of each book for specific leveling information. Penguin Young Readers features esteemed authors and illustrators, stories about favorite characters, fascinating nonfiction, and more!

Who Stole the Cookies?

LEVEL 2

GUIDED READING LEVEL **F**

This book is perfect for a **Progressing Reader** who:
• can figure out unknown words by using picture and context clues;
• can recognize beginning, middle, and ending sounds;
• can make and confirm predictions about what will happen in the text; and
• can distinguish between fiction and nonfiction.

Here are some **activities** you can do during and after reading this book:
• There is a lot of sentence structure repetition in this book: Who stole the cookies from the cookie jar? I think _____ stole the cookies from the cookie jar. Write these sentences a few times on a separate piece of paper. Then have the child think of other people or animals who could have stolen the cookies. Fill in the blanks.
• The author/illustrator of this book uses cut paper to illustrate the text. The child can use this technique, too! Once the blanks are filled in for the previous activity, have the child go through a magazine and carefully cut out a picture that illustrates the person or animal in the blank. For example, a mailman, a horse, etc.

Remember, sharing the love of reading with a child is the best gift you can give!

—Bonnie Bader, EdM, and Katie Carella, EdM
    Penguin Young Readers program

*Penguin Young Readers are leveled by independent reviewers applying the standards developed by Irene Fountas and Gay Su Pinnell in *Matching Books to Readers: Using Leveled Books in Guided Reading*, Heinemann, 1999.

For Morgan, Raisin, Minky, and Budgie

Penguin Young Readers
Published by the Penguin Group
Penguin Group (USA) Inc., 375 Hudson Street, New York, New York 10014, USA
Penguin Group (Canada), 90 Eglinton Avenue East, Suite 700,
Toronto, Ontario M4P 2Y3, Canada
(a division of Pearson Penguin Canada Inc.)
Penguin Books Ltd., 80 Strand, London WC2R 0RL, England
Penguin Group Ireland, 25 St. Stephen's Green, Dublin 2, Ireland
(a division of Penguin Books Ltd.)
Penguin Group (Australia), 250 Camberwell Road, Camberwell, Victoria 3124, Australia
(a division of Pearson Australia Group Pty. Ltd.)
Penguin Books India Pvt. Ltd., 11 Community Centre, Panchsheel Park, New Delhi—110 017, India
Penguin Group (NZ), 67 Apollo Drive, Rosedale, Auckland 0632, New Zealand
(a division of Pearson New Zealand Ltd.)
Penguin Books (South Africa) (Pty.) Ltd., 24 Sturdee Avenue, Rosebank,
Johannesburg 2196, South Africa

Penguin Books Ltd., Registered Offices: 80 Strand, London WC2R 0RL, England

Special thanks to Paul Dyer Photography.

Library of Congress Control Number: 95-20847

ISBN 978-0-448-41127-9   10 9 8 7 6 5 4 3 2 1

Who Stole the Cookies?

by Judith Moffatt

Penguin Young Readers
An Imprint of Penguin Group (USA) Inc.

Who stole the cookies

from the cookie jar?

4

I think Cat
stole the cookies
from the
cookie jar.

5

Then who?

I think Puppy

stole the cookies

from the cookie jar.

Who, me?

Yes, you.

Not me.

10

Then who?

I think Mouse

stole the cookies

from the cookie jar.

Who, me?

No, siree.

Come along.

Follow me.

I think Squirrel

stole the cookies

from the cookie jar.

Who, me,

did you say?

Not me. No way!

I think Turtle

stole the cookies

from the cookie jar.

Oh, no! Not true!

But here is a clue.

You will find

the thief in there!

Look in the cave

if you dare!

Bear stole the cookies

from the cookie jar!

I'm a very sorry bear.

But it's so hard

to share.

Don't cry.

I'll tell you why.

27

Everybody follow me!

We'll bake more cookies,

one, two, three!

Yum!

Let's have some.